W9-BJV-900

The Puppy Book

For Roxanna and Jeremy

Text copyright © 1980, 1991 by Camilla Jessel
Photographs copyright © 1980 by Camilla Jessel

All rights reserved.
First published in Great Britain in 1980 by Methuen Children's Books Ltd.

This revised edition first published in Great Britain in 1991
by Walker Books Ltd., London.

Revised edition first published in the U.S. in 1992

Library of Congress Catalog Card Number 91-71825
Library of Congress Cataloging-in-Publication Data
Jessel, Camilla.
Originally published: London:New York : Methuen, 1980.
Summary: Text and illustrations follow a retriever as she
gives birth to and cares for nine puppies.
ISBN 1-56402-021-5
1. Puppies—Juvenile literature. 2. Dogs—Parturition—Juvenile literature.
3. Labrador retriever—Juvenile literature. [1. Dogs—Reproduction.] I. Title.
SF426.5.J47   1992
636.7'07—dc20   91-71825

10 9 8 7 6 5 4 3 2

Printed and bound in Hong Kong.

Candlewick Press
2067 Massachusetts Avenue
Cambridge, Massachusetts 02140

The
Puppy Book

—by Camilla Jessel—

CANDLEWICK PRESS
CAMBRIDGE, MASSACHUSETTS

Saffy the Labrador is about to have puppies.

Since she was mated two months ago with a handsome Labrador called Bobby, her stomach has been slowly swelling. Now in the last week she is so fat she can hardly waddle. She lies down to rest for most of the day and finds it an effort to heave herself up again.

Andrew has been watching her progress carefully. Now he can feel small, jerky movements as the tiny unborn puppies move around inside their mother's womb. "Hey, that one actually jabbed me – they must be really strong!"

Saffy searches for the perfect place to have her puppies. The wolves, her ancestors, had their cubs in the forests, and some ancient instinct makes Saffy want to dig a hollow in the earth for her puppies. She chooses the prettiest flower bed in the garden. But it's the wrong kind of bed . . .

so she digs again, in a softer, more comfortable place. "Really, Saffy," scolds Andrew, "you know you're not allowed up on the sofa."

At last Saffy's special birthing box is ready. Lynn lines it with newspapers, which will make a good, warm surface for the puppies, but can be thrown out when they get dirty. Then she encourages Saffy to try it. Saffy seems delighted and inspects it each day to make sure it's still there.

A few days later Saffy makes for the birthing box. She is obviously feeling strange. She sits there shivering and starts to puff and pant. The children want to know what's happening. "Saffy is going into labor at last," explains their father. "Until the puppies are fully developed, they are held safely in their mother's womb. But when the nine weeks of pregnancy are completed, the puppies have grown strong enough to be born. Saffy's puffing and shivering are the outward signs that her muscles are slowly flexing – ready to ease the puppies out into the world. Try not to be impatient; her labor will probably last a long time."

Saffy is in labor for almost eighteen hours. All night her mistress stays quietly beside her.

In the middle of the night, instinct makes Saffy tear up all the newspaper lining her box to make it softer for her babies.

The children rush downstairs at dawn, but still no puppies have arrived.

Everyone goes to breakfast. When they come back, Saffy has disappeared. They search for her everywhere – the house, the garden, the street. They start to get seriously worried. At last Andrew cries out, "Found her!"

"Oh, no – you're not having your puppies on my new bedroom carpet!" cries the children's mother.

Lynn gently leads Saffy back to the birthing box and brings her a strengthening eggnog, a mixture of beaten egg and sugar in warm milk.

Soon Saffy starts to pant more urgently. The children leave her now, because sometimes the mother dog has difficulty giving birth to the first puppy. Having too many people around, even those she loves best, could make her nervous.

A few minutes later the children's father calls them back and tells them to stay absolutely quiet and still. The first puppy has been born and is already licked clean by its mother.

It has been placed safely under a warm towel as Saffy is about to give birth again.

Soon the next puppy appears.

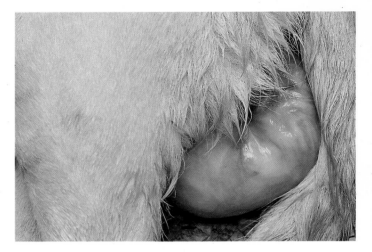

Each puppy is born in its own protective bag, which Saffy quickly bites open so the puppy can breathe. Although she has never had puppies before, she knows instinctively what to do.

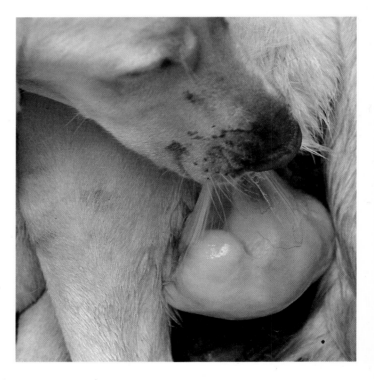

"Was I born in a bag like that?" Andrew asks his father.
"Well, human babies also float comfortably in a protective bag of fluid in their mother's womb so that they can't be bruised or squashed. But with humans, the bag breaks before they're actually born."

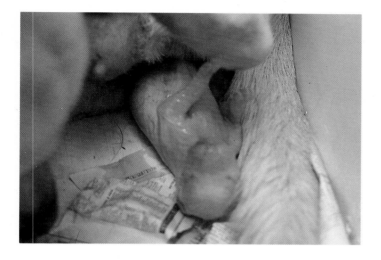

The newest puppy lies there helpless and still. Saffy licks and licks . . .

and a few moments later it's no longer slimy – the puppy begins to look absolutely hairy.

After a few more licks, within just a few minutes of birth, it is already drinking its mother's warm, strengthening milk.

There are four puppies now. Saffy is already tired, so Lynn gives her more eggnog.

More puppies come. Five, six, seven – surely that is all! But half an hour later the eighth comes, and a full three hours after the birth of the first puppy, the last is born. Saffy has nine beautiful puppies, seven males and two females, an unusually large litter, and they all seem to be strong and well.

Saffy is very proud, but extremely tired. Now she must be left in total peace with her family. The puppies have to get used to breathing in the outside world. All they need is their mother to keep them warm and give them milk.

The vet then asks Lynn and Andrew to take Saffy out for a short walk so that he can look at the puppies without upsetting her. He checks them carefully to make sure that the insides of their mouths are perfectly shaped for sucking, that their stomachs are properly formed, and their claws normal. He finds that one puppy is much larger than the rest and one is much smaller, but all are healthy and strong enough to survive.

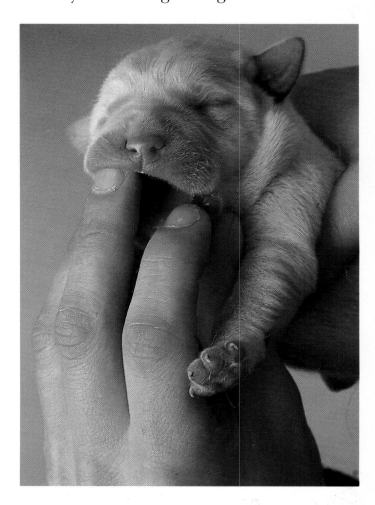

Though Saffy knows the postman well, the next morning she rushes out, barking at him fiercely. A new, protective instinct makes her think of anyone who comes to the house as an enemy who might steal her puppies.

Later Saffy's old friend the vet arrives. Again the hair rises along her neck and she growls angrily. Eventually she senses that he means no harm, and she sits down quietly while he feels her stomach.

The puppies' skins are loose and full of wrinkles. "Plenty of room to grow into," says Lynn. "I wonder how long they will take to fill out."

Saffy needs a few short walks each day, and the puppies feel cold without her. For the first two weeks they cannot shiver, which would help to warm them. (They are also unable to pant, which is the way dogs cool themselves.) So while their mother is away, they huddle together for warmth.

For at least two weeks the puppies hate being picked up. They feel unsafe, however carefully and gently they are held. They wriggle and struggle. They aren't yet ready to make friends with human beings.

They still want only their mother.

Human babies have wide-open, staring eyes at birth, though they can see only hazily. Puppies are born with their eyes tightly shut.

When a puppy wants to feed, it sways its nose to and fro until it touches its mother's paw. Then, by scrabbling along her legs, it can find it's way to the food.

After about eight or nine days black dots appear in the corner of its eyes . . .

and three or four days later its eyes are completely open, though it can see only mistily for many days after that.

While human babies take about a year to learn to walk, puppies are on their feet in three weeks.

The first week their legs cannot hold them up at all. They slither along looking more like baby seals than dogs.

After a few more days they can get their legs under them.

A week later they can almost walk, though their weak, wobbly legs bend under the weight of their bodies.

At three weeks they can stand straight and tall; at one month they run and jump. If the weather is good, they may go outside.

Although Saffy is given extra food and vitamins, she is tired from feeding her puppies. There is not enough room for all nine to eat at the same time, and they battle against one another to suck. The feedings seem to last for ages, and then they start again in two to three hours.

Usually the mother has enough milk to satisfy her puppies completely until they are three weeks old. However, because Saffy has such a large litter, the puppies already need milky cereal at two weeks. At first Lynn has to teach each one to lick the food off her fingers.

They love it. In no time they learn to lap from their bowls, though they're not very tidy eaters.

At one month they can manage easily, and their meals seem to disappear in seconds . . .

though they still get much of their food from their mother.

Puppies seem to develop the instinct to fight almost as soon as they can stand, but they don't hurt one another, as they haven't yet cut any teeth.

They all have the instinct to explore. The bravest puppy attempts the first expedition outside the walls of the birthing box, which has been their whole world for their first three weeks. He heaves himself out over the ledge to investigate the dark room beyond, but he soon turns around and tries to get back to his brothers and sisters.

Once the puppies are old enough to spend the warm hours of the day in the garden, they discover numerous exciting new smells and learn not to bump their noses tumbling off high steps.

While the puppies are cutting their teeth, they try to chew whatever they find but quickly realize that not everything crumples at their bite.

Water is another puzzling experience, as up until now the puppies' only drink has been their mother's milk.

Puppies learn by their mistakes. Hoping for an extra feed, the greediest one knocks over the jug their breakfast came in and gets stuck.

The puppies keep growing fast. At five weeks they play more with their mother but need less of her milk. Now they eat hamburger meat with gravy-soaked biscuits.

The largest puppy eats faster than the rest. He often manages to push a smaller one away and grab two dinners.

Lynn and Andrew worry that the same puppy might be missing its food every time, so they decide to mark all of them with different colored ribbons. Then they will be able to tell if any puppy needs extra care.

Once each puppy has its own ribbon, the children realize how different their characters are.

Pink is gentle, sensitive, and often the victim who loses her food to greedy Blue.

Orange is a champion chewer and is always discovering new toys to bite. Yellow follows her around all the time, ready to join her in play.

Green is rather sad and shy. He creeps off on his own and watches the world from behind the spiky iris leaves. He is nervous around strangers and scared even of his own brothers and sisters.

Andrew decides to give him plenty of extra love and care.

This works well. Green's confidence grows, and after two weeks of special attention he is even seen leading some of the others in an escape.

But the naughtiest and most adventurous puppy is Red. "We chose his ribbon well," Andrew remarks. "Red for danger!"

It is Red who squeezes beneath the gate into the chicken coop, though he does not like the cackling, curious hens when he gets there.

It is Red who tries to catch a goldfish, falls into the pond, and has to be wrapped in a warm towel so he will not catch a cold.

It is Red who climbs onto the trash heap and makes himself all smelly. ·

And it is Red who scrambles up onto the kitchen table after lunch and eats one roll and two jam tarts, then drinks some orange juice from a glass.

The puppies are growing more independent. Though they play rough-and-tumble games with their mother, they hardly feed from her at all. Now they need human companionship – people of their own to love and guard.

Lynn and Andrew hate the thought of parting with any of the puppies. "But we can't keep them all," says their father. "Imagine ten full-grown Labradors running around the house – there wouldn't be any room for us. And think of how much food they'd eat!"

The first puppy leaves home at just six weeks. He is bought by a family whose old dog has recently died. Nine-year-old John has been desperately missing his pet. He chooses Purple, a friendly, affectionate puppy. "Purple will soon stop John from feeling sad," comments Lynn, but she feels miserable for a moment as the new owners' car drives away.

The next to go is greedy Blue. He is bought by two ladies who have a cottage with a garden for him. "Blue is so bossy," laughs Andrew, "I think he will own them instead of their owning him."

Pink, Orange, Yellow, Black, and Brown go to new homes during the next week. Lynn and Andrew manage to hide their favorites, Red and Green. They want to keep both puppies for themselves, as well as Saffy, but their parents say that one big dog in the house is enough.

Then two friendly-looking boys come along. "They look just right," says Andrew. "Anyway, there's nothing we can do about it – either Red or Green will have to go."

Jason and Adam find it hard to choose, but in the end they take Green.

Saffy doesn't mind too much. She still has one puppy to play with.

Jason and Adam promise to telephone to say how Green has settled in. They decide to call him Gringo because it sounds like Green.

Gringo doesn't seem upset at leaving. It is quite natural for a puppy of his age to forget his mother and the other puppies. He enjoys the fuss and attention from his new family, who cuddles and strokes him all the way home. When they arrive, Adam and Jason show him every corner of their house and garden. Gringo finds lots of interesting new sights and smells, and he loves chasing balls and playing with the boys.

The first night Gringo feels strange with no other puppies to cuddle up against. Adam makes him comfortable in a box beside his bed, with a hot-water bottle under the blanket and a clock ticking to sound like Saffy's heartbeat.

Early in the morning the sleepy puppy is lifted from his bed and taken straight to the yard before he has a chance to urinate in the house. The boys are delighted when he urinates outside. They have been told that the best way to train their puppy is to praise him when he is good and scold him – not spank him – when he is naughty.

Gringo wants to please his two young masters very much. As they brush him, feed him, and care for him, he learns to love and trust them more deeply every day. He feels safe with them, and he tries to be good and understand what they are training him to do.

Their baby brother also needs to be trained. He must learn to pat and hug the puppy gently.

Sometimes Gringo is bad, though he doesn't mean to be. When he sees the baby playing with a tasty-looking toy, he thinks he will try to eat it . . .

and the baby likes to chew Gringo's rubber bone. This is not a good idea, as there could be something unhealthy in the puppy's saliva that could make the baby ill.

As Gringo cuts more teeth, he needs to chew to help them through his gums. After he has chewed the arm off Jason's robot and bitten both eyes off Adam's bear, the boys go to the butcher and ask for a bone. He gives them a large shin bone, which will not chip or get stuck in their puppy's throat.

Gringo gradually finds that he can understand the words the boys are teaching him. He takes only a few minutes to learn the order to sit, because he is given a dog biscuit every time he obeys. He soon starts to come when he is called, especially at dinner time.

Leash training doesn't go so well at first. Gringo hates being pulled along by his neck. He just sits down and looks sadly at Adam.

Jason goes to the other end of the yard and tries waving a tempting biscuit. At once Gringo gets the idea of trotting "at heel" in order to reach his reward.

Because the boys are kind and patient, Gringo will soon be one of the best-trained puppies around. But of course he's naughty sometimes too!

In the meantime, who has bought
mischievous Red?

No one, because Andrew and Lynn have
persuaded their parents to let them keep
him after all.